SUPER ROOSTER
AND WONDER CAT

By
Alma Hammond

Illustrated by
Hugh Keiser

SWEETBEET BOOKS

Bethesda, Maryland

Book and cover design by Sagaponack Books & Design
Map design by Ralph Scherer, Scherer Media
Author's photograph by Aliyah Dastour

ISBNs:
978-0-9985362-0-0 (soft-cover)
978-0-9985362-2-4 (hardcover)
978-0-9985362-2-1 (ebook)

Library of Congress Control Number: 2017907372

Summary: Set in Bora Bora in French Polynesia, Super Rooster and Wonder Cat ramble down to the lagoon to practice their super powers. There they meet up with sea creatures living on and in the lagoon that have very special super powers of their own.

JUV002170 Juvenile Fiction / Animals / Marine Life
JUV039060 Juvenile Fiction / Social Themes / Friendship
JUV039140 Juvenile Fiction / Self-Esteem & Self-Reliance
JUV002050 Juvenile Fiction / Animals / Cats
JUV001000 Juvenile Fiction / Animals / General

Printed and bound in the United States of America

First Edition

To my husband Bob.
I can't wait to visit Rooster, Cat,
and Bora Bora again soon.

*We are each gifted in a unique and important way.
It is our privilege and our adventure to discover our
own special light.*

—Mary Dunbar

Nearly every sunrise, best friends Rooster and Cat rambled down to the lagoon to practice their superpowers. The beautiful, sandy beach by crystal-clear waters provided the perfect place to show off their talents.

One morning, Rooster began to practice what he called his Cockadoodle Dazzle. With a single *cock-a-doodle-doo*, he could draw the attention of every living creature on and in the lagoon. "Cock-a-doodle-doo—a-doodle-doo—a-doodle-doo," Rooster crowed. He strutted along the beach, gazing at the creatures he attracted. "Now you try, Cat," said Rooster.

"I can't Cockledoodle Dazzle as well as you, Super Rooster," said Cat. "But I can climb that coconut tree lickety-split and get us a coconut." Cat scurried up the tree and knocked down the biggest coconut. *Kerplunk*! A giant coconut hit the ground. "Wow, Wonder Cat!" Rooster exclaimed.

Just then, a strange creature crawled by with large pincers for hands.

"Who are you?" asked Cat.

"I am Crab," said Crab.

"OO-OO," said Rooster.

"Hiss," said Cat.

"Don't be afraid, Rooster and Cat," Crab told them. "I only use my pincers to defend and feed myself. As long as you're careful not to touch me or step on me, we can all enjoy the lagoon."

"Yes, we certainly will be careful," Cat agreed.

"So, what is your superpower, Crab?" Rooster asked.

"I can't Cockadoodle Dazzle or climb a tree as fast as you, Cat," Crab said, "but I can do this...."

Crab picked up a fallen coconut and cracked it open with its giant claw.

"Wow!" said Cat.

"Wow!" said Rooster.

Suddenly, a strange-looking fish, with wings for fins and white spots all over, surfaced out of the water.

"Who are you?" asked Rooster.

"I am Ray," said Ray.

"OO-OO," said Rooster.

"Hiss," said Cat.

"Don't be afraid, Rooster and Cat," Ray assured them. "I only use my stinger to defend myself. As long as you're careful not to touch me or step on me, we can all enjoy the lagoon."

"Yes, we certainly will be careful," Rooster agreed.

"So, what is your superpower, Ray?" Cat asked.

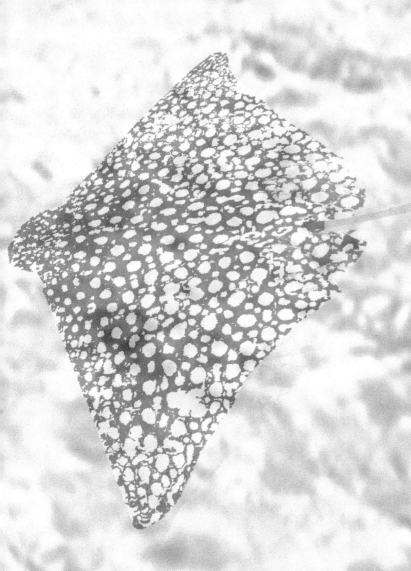

"I can't Cockadoodle Dazzle, climb a tree, or crack open coconuts, but I can fly like a bird right out of the water," said Ray. Ray then hurled himself into the air, flapping his wing-like fins before landing with a large belly flop.

"Wow!" said Cat.

"Wow!" said Rooster.

SPLASH! Another strange fish popped out of the water.
"Who are you?" Rooster asked.
"I am Shark," said Shark.
"OO-OO," said Rooster.
"Hiss," said Cat.

"Don't be afraid, Rooster and Cat. I only bite to defend myself or capture food. As long as you're careful not to touch me or step on me, we can all enjoy the lagoon," said Shark.

"Yes, we certainly will be careful," said Cat.

"So, what is your superpower, Shark?" asked Rooster.

"I'm not one for cock-a-doodling, climbing, cracking coconuts, or flying like a bird, but I can do a high jump out of the water," said Shark. Shark then swam with incredible speed before jumping several feet out of the water.

"Wow!" said Cat.

"Wow!" said Rooster.

The sun finally set, and Cat
and Rooster made their way home
to the farm.

The next sunrise, Cat and Rooster headed down to the lagoon to watch their new sea creature friends practice their superpowers.

On the shore, a cast of crabs carried coconuts as large as themselves to a safe place for cracking.

Just off the shore, a school of rays launched into the air flapping their wings.

And a shiver of sharks, jumping out of the water, created
a majestic fountain.

"Ooh," said Super Rooster.
"Aah," said Wonder Cat.
The two companions were mesmerized by their new friends' superpowers!

Ask Yourself:

Whose superpower did you like best and why?

What is your superpower?

What are your friends' superpowers?

For Practice:

Try a Cock-a-doodle-Dazzle:

Cock-a-doodle-Doo~A-Doodle-Doo ~A-Doodle-Doo!

Bora Bora is an island of French Polynesia located in the South Pacific, 160 miles northwest of Tahiti and about 2,600 miles South of Hawaii.

Coconut crabs, spotted eagle rays, and black tip reef sharks can be found around and in lagoons of the island of Bora Bora.

Fun Facts:

Coconut crabs do eat coconuts. To get to the meat, they scrape off the husk, stab them at a weak point, and rip them open.

Coconut crabs are a type of hermit crab. They can weigh up to 9 pounds and grow up to 3 feet, 3 inches long.

Coconut crabs can live for more than 50 years.

It is believed spotted eagle rays jump out of the water to avoid a predator chasing them.

A school of spotted eagle rays most often consists of six or more rays swimming in the same direction at the same speed.

Spotted eagle rays can grow up to 8 feet long, over 16 feet long if you include the tail.

The black tip reef shark can jump fully out of the water, often during feeding frenzies.

Black tip reef sharks often appear in shallow coastal waters near reefs.

In Hawaii, some families see black tip reef sharks as being a "Guardian Spirit."

Alma Hammond came up the idea for this book while on her honeymoon in Bora Bora. Every morning she would witness a cat and rooster playing together on the beach, an unlikely but fun friendship. She also observed many amazing sea creatures at close range. Alma Hammond lives with her husband Bob, two cats Violet and Daisy, and dog Stazi in Bethesda, Maryland. This is Alma Hammond's first book.

Hugh Keiser has been a professional artist working in a variety of mediums for over forty-five years. His award-winning art is displayed in public and private collections around the world. A love and appreciation for art, nature, and children led Hugh to create children's book illustrations. Hugh lives in St. Augustine, Florida, with his wife Frances and three inquisitive cats, Tina, Toby, and Simba.

CPSIA information can be obtained
at www.ICGtesting.com
Printed in the USA
BVOW05s1001230717
489690BV00010B/89/P

9 780998 536200